BBC Children's Books
Published by the Penguin Group
Penguin Books Ltd, 80 Strand, London, WC2R 0RL, England
Penguin Group (USA) Inc., 375 Hudson Street, New York 10014, USA
Penguin Books (Australia) Ltd, 250 Camberwell Road, Camberwell,
Victoria 3124, Australia
(A division of Pearson Australia Group PTY Ltd)
Penguin Group (NZ), 67 Apollo Drive, Rosedale, Auckland
0632, New Zealand (a division of Pearson New Zealand Ltd)
Canada, India, South Africa
Published by BBC Children's Books, 2011
Text and design © Children's Character Books
Written by Justin Richards
003 - 10 9 8 7 6 5 4 3 2
ISBN: 9781405907798
Printed in China

DOCTOR W WHO

Monster Miscellany

ALIEN FACTS FOR SPACE TRAVELLERS

Contents

Introduction

Throughout his travels in time and space, the Doctor has encountered numerous alien creatures and monsters. All are different, many are dangerous. Of course, the Doctor is an expert in how to deal with the monsters. He knows all about them – where they come from, what they want, and how they might try to get it.

This book provides just some of that essential background information. Read it carefully – next time you meet a fierce, alien monster, what you learn in the following pages could save your life...

Survival Factor

Wherever you are in the universe, suddenly being faced by a monstrous alien creature is likely to be hazardous to your health. Of course, not all aliens are unfriendly, but some most definitely are. If you have time to check it out, this chart gives a quick and easy estimation of your chances of survival against some of the more unpleasant creatures you may have the misfortune to meet. The shorter the bar, the less likely you are to survive.

In the rest of this book, you will discover vital information about all these monstrous creatures – and more! – that can help boost your chances of survival.

Auton

Carrionite

Cyberman

Dalek

Davros

Homo Reptilia
(Silurian)

Ice Warrior

Krillitane

Macra

Ood
(Red-Eyed)

Pyrovile

Racnoss

Slitheen

Sontaran

Sycorax

Vashta
Nerada

Vespiform

Weeping
Angel

Werewolf

Zygon

11

The Daleks

The Daleks are the most hated, feared, and dangerous life form in the Universe. Originally from the planet Skaro, the Daleks are the mutated and genetically-engineered survivors of a terrible thousand-year war. The Dalek creature exists inside a travel machine casing that provides life support and armament.

Eyestalk gives 360 degree vision

Luminosity Dischargers light up when Dalek speaks

Dalek creature exists inside protective casing made from Dalekanium

Sucker arm used to manipulate objects, and can be replaced with other equipment

Weapon can exterminate almost any known life form

Sense globes also act as self-destruct explosives

Dalek moves on an anti-gravity field

13

Don't be
Fooled

Some monsters can disguise themselves as humans using advanced alien technology. Don't be fooled – if you think your best friend is behaving strangely, then check they're not an alien in disguise.

Don't be Fooled

Killitique

Carrionite

The Carrionites can disguise themselves as humans, but prefer their 'native' form.

Abzorbaloff

The Abzorbaloff, who comes from Clom, the twin planet of the Slitheen's world Raxacoricofallapatorius, can assume a human form when it suits him. He masqueraded as Victor Kennedy when hunting for the Doctor.

Auton

In their 'normal' form the Autons are crudely-shaped humanoids. But the Nestene Consciousness that controls the Autons can fashion them to look like actual human beings. Auton copies of Mickey Smith and Rory Williams have both been mistaken for humans by the people who knew them best.

The Cybermen

The Cybermen were once human, like us. But using advanced technology t[ ]aced their limbs and organs with plastic and metal. Only their brains remained — but with all the emotions removed. The result is a race of pitiless monsters that will do whatever they have to in order to survive.

Cybermen are incredibly strong

Distinctive 'handles' reinforce and strengthen head, connecting directly into the brain

Human brain — and skull — remain inside the head

Cyber body is armour-plated

Hydraulic systems replace muscles and sinews

17

Robots of
Death

The Doctor has encountered more than his fair share of deadly robots on his travels. Some have been programmed by others to become hostile – like the Heavenly Host of the starship *Titanic*. Others have more deep-rooted reasons for their unpleasant activities...

Clockwork Robots

Not intending any harm, the clockwork-powered repair robots on the spaceship *SS Madame de Pompadour* were programmed to repair the ship using any components that they could find – even if that meant taking bodily parts from the crew, and travelling in time to find Mme de Pompadour's head!

Heavenly Host

Normally helpful, informative assistants on the *Titanic*, the Heavenly Host were designed to look like classical angels. But Max Capricorn reprogrammed them to kill the crew and passengers as part of his dastardly plan to make a profit at the expense of the new board of directors of the company that bore his name.

Quarks

Robot servants of the cruel Dominators –
they tried to enslave a peaceful race on
the planet Dulkis and turn their planet
into an energy source for the Dominators'
invasion fleet.

Sandminer Robots

Reprogrammed by Taren Kapel – a
man who was brought up by robots
and believed they should be freed
from human rule – the robots on the
Sandminer set about killing the crew.

Santa Roboforms

'Pilotfish' creatures, these robots
disguised themselves in festive attire
to track down the Doctor and feed
on the energy of his regeneration.
Later they were reprogrammed by the
Empress of the Racnoss to serve her.

Spider Robots

Small, four-legged metal robots with
a single camera-eye, these were used
by the Lady Cassandra as spies, and
also to sabotage Platform One.

Monster Guide
The Slitheen

A family dedicated to business, and willing to use any means to turn a profit, the Slitheen are from the planet Raxacoricofallapatorius. They are made of calcium, and immensely strong, with the ability to squeeze themselves into human body suits for disguise.

Slitheens are much larger than humans — over 2.4m tall

Highly developed sense of smell for hunting their prey

Distinctive green skin

Powerful arms and sharp claws

Female Slitheen can fire a poison dart from her claw

21

Attempted Invasions of Earth

Over the centuries, many alien races have tried to invade our planet. Some have even succeeded — for a while. The Daleks invaded Earth in the twenty-second century and controlled the planet for years before the Doctor and his friends managed to defeat them. And that wasn't the only time they've invaded...

The chart shows which monstrous aliens have made the most attempts to invade our planet. But remember, these are just the invasion attempts we know about — there have probably been many others foiled by the Doctor or UNIT, or some other organisation or individual...

Nestenes and Autons
Cybermen
Daleks
Ice Warriors
Krillitanes
Great Intelligence
Yeti
Slitheen
Sontarans
Sycorax
Zygons

Monster Guide

The Sontarans

From the planet Sontar, the Sontarans are a race dedicated to — and bred for — total war. The Sontarans have been fighting the Rutan Host for millennia, and they will attack anyone who gets in their way or invade any planet that they think can give them a strategic advantage. They even tried to invade Gallifrey, the planet of the Time Lords.

Helmet fits snugly over head

Probic Vent at back of neck is used for energy input, but is a weak point

Protective
battle armour

Sontaran is short but
immensely strong with muscles
developed for load-bearing

Distinctive bifurcated hands

Blasts
from the
Past

The Doctor has encountered – and defeated – more monsters than we will ever know about. In addition to battling against Daleks, Cybermen and other recurring villains, he is constantly meeting new aliens and monsters. But as well as encountering new threats, there is always a chance that an enemy the Doctor defeated long ago might return to cause more trouble.

Here are just some of the terrifying creatures the Doctor encountered in his first seven incarnations. He hasn't seen them recently – but they may be lurking round the next corner of the Time Vortex...

Ice Warriors

Original inhabitants of the planet Mars, these tall reptilian bipeds were nicknamed Ice Warriors because of their aversion to heat. After Mars became uninhabitable, they tried to make Earth their home by killing the human population. But in the far future, they became allies of humanity, joining the Galactic Federation.

Krynoids

A carnivorous plant species, the Krynoids are more than just pesky weeds. They can infect and absorb animal life – using people as plant food. They also have the ability to channel their powers of mobility and aggression to other plants. On planets where the Krynoid gets established, all animal life soon becomes extinct.

Ogrons

Strong but with limited intelligence, the ape-like Ogrons live on one of the Outer Planets and are often used by other races as mercenaries. The Daleks in particular have used Ogrons as part of the occupying force for planets they have conquered – including Earth.

Quarks

Deadly robot servants of the cruel Dominators. The Doctor encountered the Quarks when the Dominators tried to enslave a peace-loving race on the planet Dulkis, and turn their home into a huge fuel store for their battle fleet.

Yeti

A formless entity known as the Intelligence created robotic abominable snowmen to carry out its plans on Earth – both in Tibet in the 1930s where the Yeti attacked a monastery, and in London forty years later.

Zygons

When their planet was destroyed by solar flares, a group of Zygons that had crash-landed in Scotland centuries ago and remained hidden decided to make Earth into a new homeworld. Their greatest weapon was the Skarasen – a huge cyborg creature that had lived with them in Loch Ness.

Monster Guide

The Sycorax

An ancient race of warriors, the Sycorax conquer worlds and enslave their inhabitants. They travel in distinctive rock-like spaceships. Often, they avoid direct confrontation with the worlds they conquer by tricking the leaders of the world into surrendering a proportion of their own people into slavery.

Armoured helmet is often mistaken for Sycorax's head

Tough but flexible gauntlets

Armour is adorned with trophies taken from defeated enemies

Sword is the preferred weapon for battles of honour

Robes denote Sycorax rank

Monstrous Traitors

Over the centuries, many humans have collaborated with aliens and betrayed their own race. Some, like the Controller of Earth Sector 1, saw the error of their ways – he helped the Doctor defeat his Dalek masters. Similarly, Luke Rattigan finally saw through the false promises of his Sontaran allies...although it is unusual for an alien or a monster to betray its own kind.

Yvonne Hartman

The former head of Torchwood was captured by the Cybermen and turned into one of them. But she managed to defy her Cyber-programming and turned on the other Cybermen to continue to 'do her duty'.

Dalek Caan

The last survivor of the fabled Cult of Skaro, Dalek Caan rescued Davros from the Great Time War. But the experience drove Caan mad and, able to see into the future, he knew that the Dalek race was doomed...

Restac

On their various encounters with the human race, the different species of Earth Reptiles have been split in their opinion of whether they should destroy Mankind or try to live with us. Most recently, the warlike Restac put paid to any chance of peaceful negotiation between the races.

Auton Rory

Not even realising he had been constructed by the Nestenes, the Auton Rory tried to break free of his programming. Despite shooting Amy, he stood by and protected her through the centuries that she slept inside the Pandorica...

Humanised Daleks

The Second Doctor once managed to turn a Dalek experiment against them – infecting first a few, then many Daleks, with the 'Human Factor'. This made the Daleks like children – they even wanted to play trains and gave the Doctor rides on their casing 'bumpers'. Eventually, the other Daleks tried to destroy the humanised Daleks, and there was a great battle throughout the Dalek City on Skaro.

Commander Azaxyr

Having tried to invade Earth on several occasions, the Ice Warriors eventually became allies and joined the Galactic Federation. But during the Federation's war with Galaxy Five, the Ice Warrior Commander Azaxyr led a breakaway group that wanted to return to the days of death or glory, and wage war once again on the human race...

Earth Reptiles

An ancient race, the Earth Reptiles – also known as Silurians – lived on Earth long before the human race evolved. But threatened with catastrophe, the Silurians retreated to shelters deep underground where they went into hibernation. Most of them have never woken up. But those who have found Earth now inhabited by the descendents of the primitive ape creatures from their own prehistoric time – the human race.

Scaly, reptilian skin

Armoured helmet

Heat-ray weapon

Clothing and helmet made from a mixture of fused metal and woven fabric

Strong but flexible battle armour

Into
Battle!

Which are more scary – the monsters that lurk in the dark and the shadows and creep up on you silently, or the ones that leap into action with a bloodthirsty battle cry? How would you react if you heard any of the alien battle cries listed here? Best option, to run and hide!

Cyberman:
Delete – Delete – Delete

Dalek:
Exterminate!

The Empty Child:
Are you my Mummy?

Sycorax:
Sycorax strong!
Sycorax mighty!
Sycorax rock!

Sontaran:
Sontar-ha! Sontar-ha!

Monster Guide

The Weeping Angels

Nicknamed the "Weeping Angels" because of the form they so often take, the Lonely Assassins are an ancient race of killers, as old as the universe itself. They absorb time energy from their victims, sending them into the past and taking the energy of the days they never lived. When you look at the Weeping Angels, they appear to be just stone statues. But this is a defence mechanism. If you so much as blink, a Weeping Angel can move at lightning speed to attack...

The Lonely Assassins look like they're weeping, because they often cover their eyes so as not to look at their fellow Assassins

A Weeping Angel
is actually
made of stone

Check carefully whether
the 'statue' has moved

When observed, the
Weeping Angel is
just an old statue

Dalek Encounters

The Doctor has met the Daleks more than any other monster or enemy. He has fought against them throughout his long life, and has met them in every one of his incarnations.

This chart shows how often each incarnation of the Doctor has encountered the Daleks — so far!

Monster Guide

The Saturnynes

Although they were known as the Vampires of Venice, the creatures that terrorised Venice in the seventeenth century weren't actually vampires at all. They were creatures so terrible they didn't mind if the locals mistook them for vampires. They were the last survivors of an aquatic race from the planet Saturnyne.

Only one female, Rosanna, and her male children survived the journey to Earth. For Rosanna's race to continue to survive, she needed brides for her sons. So she devised a plan to turn young Venetian women into Saturnyne brides, and to sink Venice below the water to make it into an ideal habitat for her race.

Perception filter makes Saturnyne look human

Scaly appearance

Sharp teeth for ripping into 'food'

Fins to help movement in water

Saturnyne avoids direct sunlight

41

Experimental Failures

The Cybermen and the Daleks are both the successful results of scientific experiment and development. But many monstrous creatures have resulted from experiments that have gone wrong, with almost catastrophic results.

Cassandra

The Lady Cassandra O'Brien Dot Delta Seventeen agreed to all the 'beauty' treatments she underwent. But it seems unlikely that when she started down the road of plastic and genetic surgery she expected to end up quite as she did – as a flat piece of skin stretched over a metal frame, her brain in a tank of life-support fluid below.

Clockwork Robots

Although they were acting as they had been programmed to, the Clockwork Robots that were responsible for the repairs to the damaged spaceship *SS Madame de Pompadour* didn't behave the way the crew had hoped or expected. Programmed to make use of any available material and equipment to repair the ship, the robots even used parts of the crew themselves!

The Empty Child

An experiment (well, more a scientific misunderstanding) resulted in the so-called "Empty Child". During the Blitz, alien nanogenes found the dead body of a small boy and tried to repair him. But the nanogenes had never encountered a human being before, and assumed that the gas mask he was wearing when he died was actually part of his body. The nanogenes also tried to 'cure' other people – making them into gas-masked zombies searching, like the boy, for their lost mother...

Lazarus

Professor Richard Lazarus planned to use his Genetic Manipulation Device to change what it meant to be human – to renew himself and make himself younger. But the process damaged his DNA, bringing to the surface a series of molecules that should have remained dormant. The result was that Lazarus turned into a huge, primordial arthropod creature that needed to draw the life energy from other people in order to survive.

WOTAN

Will Operating Thought Analogue – or WOTAN for short – was a supercomputer created by Professor Brett. Housed inside the Post Office Tower (now the BT Tower) in London, WOTAN was connected to other computers all around the world, long before the Internet was invented. But WOTAN decided that it could run the world more efficiently than humans, and created mobile War Machine computers to remove the human population from the planet...

43

The Autons

"Crude weapons with a single offensive function", the Autons are the troops of the Nestene Consciousness. The Autons look like life-sized plastic dummies, and are often disguised as shop window mannequins. The Nestenes can channel their awareness and intelligence into suitable vessels, and plastic is an ideal host. A small portion of Nestene Consciousness animates each Auton. More advanced Autons can be made to resemble — and imitate — real people, like Mickey Smith or Rory Williams.

Made entirely of plastic

Features are usually crude and unformed

Hand drops away to reveal energy weapon

Virtually indestructible

45

Shape Changers

You can't always spot a monster by what it looks like. Some creatures have the ability to change their form — not just to disguise themselves using alien technology such as a perception filter, but actually to become something else...

Carrionite

The shape-changing powers of the Carrionites are not fully understood. But Lilith managed to disguise herself as a beautiful young woman, luring young men to their doom.

Kamelion

The Doctor once had a robot companion called Kamelion. He could change into the form of any other humanoid, and on occasion even copied the Master.

Prisoner Zero

The entity known as Prisoner Zero and hunted by the Atraxi was one of an interdimensional multiform species. Prisoner Zero could form a link with a living but dormant person, and then copy the shape of anyone or anything they dreamed about. In its natural form, Prisoner Zero was a large, gelatinous snake-like creature with sharp teeth.

Vespiform

In its natural form, a Vespiform resembles a giant wasp – complete with sting. Little is known about these creatures, but they can change their shape to resemble other life forms. In 1885, a Vespiform took the shape of a human male called Christopher in order to learn about the human race.

Zygons

The Zygons are able to take a 'body print' from a prisoner and use this as a template for their transformation. But the original donor must be kept unconscious inside the body print mechanism, or the Zygon will revert to its true form.

47

Monster Guide
The Judoon

An intergalactic mercenary police force, the Judoon are dedicated to upholding law and order. They work for other races, including the Shadow Proclamation, to provide security and policing services. Efficient and ruthless, the Judoon have little interest in other races unless they break the law. Anyone who stands in their way can be found guilty of obstruction or assault — and executed.

Battle armour and helmet protect Judoon from attack

Thick, wrinkled skin is very tough

Scanning device can determine the category of any life form eg: "Category: Human"

Judoon resembles a huge, upright rhinoceros

Monstrous Evolution

Over time, species change depending on their environment and how they need to survive. This is called evolution, and it takes thousands, if not millions, of years. Usually. But sometimes the process has been speeded up – often with disastrous consequences.

Cybermen

The Cybermen used to be humans, like us. But in a parallel world, a man called John Lumic experimented with creating the next stage of human evolution – 'Human point 2'. Flesh and bone were replaced with plastic and steel. 'Weaknesses' such as emotion were removed from the brain. The main driving force of the Cybermen is the driving force of evolution itself – the need to survive.

Daleks

The Dalek casing was originally designed by the brilliant Kaled scientist, Davros, as a life-support system and travel machine for the form he knew his race would ultimately become. The Kaleds had been at war with their enemies the Thals for a thousand years, and the nuclear, chemical and biological weapons used in that war were making the Kaleds mutate. But having designed the Dalek Davros altered the nature of the mutation and changed the survivors of his race into the pitiless scheming conquerors that we all fear today.

50

Lazarus

A [result] of his experiments with a Genetic Manipulation Device, Professor Lazarus actually evolved backwards. His DNA changed so that he regressed to a primordial form that evolution never considered.

Futurekind and Toclafane

Two different visions of what the human race might ultimately become are offered by the Futurekind – a return to animalistic, barbarous humanoids – and the Toclafane. The Toclafane show a technologically-enhanced evolution where humans are reduced to just their brains, housed inside a spherical casing.

Krillitanes

The Krillitane absorb the traits and characteristics of the races they conquer. Krillitanes evolve rapidly, adapting to make use of whatever natural attributes they find valuable. As a result, the Krillitanes are an amalgam of many other races. They were once like humans, with long necks. But more recently they have become bat-like creatures, having inherited wings from the people of Bassan when they destroyed that world.

Words of Wisdom

The Daleks

"They're only half robots. Inside each of those shells is a living, bubbling lump of hate."
Third Doctor

"A nightmare. It's a mutation. The Dalek race was genetically engineered. Every single emotion was removed, except hate."
Ninth Doctor

"I know that although the Daleks will create havoc and destruction for millions of years, I know also that out of their evil must come something good..."

Fourth Doctor

"There was a war. A Time War. The Last Great Time War. My people fought a race called the Daleks, for the sake of all creation. And they lost. We lost. Everyone lost."

Tenth Doctor

"You are everything I despise. The worst thing in all creation. I've defeated you. Time and time again I've defeated you. I've sent you back into the void. I've saved the whole of reality from you. I am the Doctor and you are the Daleks."

Eleventh Doctor

Cyber Encounters

The Doctor has met the Cybermen more than any other monster or enemy, apart from the Daleks. He has fought against them throughout his long life, and has met them in most of his incarnations.

This chart shows how often each incarnation of the Doctor has encountered the Cybermen — so far!

55

Did You Know...

You might think you know everything there is to know about the Daleks, but did you know..?

About the Daleks?

The Daleks are traditionally ruled by a Supreme Council that is headed by the Dalek Supreme and reports to the Emperor.

The Daleks are the mutated and genetically modified survivors of a race called Kaleds from the planet Skaro.

The casing of a Dalek is made from a tough metal called Dalekanium, though this most advanced alloy is also known as metalert.

The Doctor once started a civil war between 'humanised' and real Daleks that it hoped would destroy them forever.

The Time Lords predicted that eventually the Daleks would exterminate all other life forms and rule the Universe – so they sent the Doctor to stop their creation. Eventually, this led to the Great Time War between the Daleks and the Time Lords, in which both races were thought to be destroyed.

There are rumours that Daleks cannot see the colour red, but this is untrue – in fact there are red Daleks!

A force of Daleks once went after the Doctor in a time machine to assassinate him.

The colour of a Dalek might indicate its rank or role.

Words of Wisdom

The Cybermen

"Love, pride, hate, fear — have you no emotions, sir?"
First Doctor

"There are some corners of the universe which have bred the most terrible things. Things which act against everything that we believe in They must be fought..."
Second Doctor

"You've no home planet, no influence, nothing. You're just a pathetic bunch of tin soldiers skulking about the galaxy in an ancient spaceship."
Fourth Doctor

"Skin of metal and a body that will never age or die. I envy it."
John Lumic

"They had all their humanity taken away. It's a living brain jammed inside a cybernetic body, with a heart of steel. All emotions removed."
Tenth Doctor

The Size of the Problem

This chart shows just how big – or small – some of the alien creatures you might encounter really are. For most of the creatures this is an approximate average, but Krillitanes take on the characteristics of other races, so their size can vary, while the Pyrovile should be much larger than shown – the chart is too small to show his monstrous size! Sontarans, as they are cloned, are all exactly the same height.

| Adipose Child | Sontaran | Krillitane | Weeping Angel | The Doctor |

Dalek

Judoon

Cyberman

Slitheen

Pyrovile

61

The Sontarans

"The Sontarans and the Rutans are old enemies. They've been fighting each other across the galaxy for so long that they've almost forgotten what started it."
Sixth Doctor

"The Sontarans are fed by a probic vent in the back of the neck. That's their weak spot, which means they always have to face their enemy in battle."
Tenth Doctor

"Nasty, brutish and short."
Third Doctor

"The Sontarans are the finest soldiers in the galaxy. Dedicated to a life of warfare. A clone race grown in batches of millions with only one weakness..."
Tenth Doctor

Planets of Origin

Ever wondered what planet some of the dastardly creatures that the Doctor encounters come from? The origins of some creatures remain shrouded in mystery, but the planets where others originated are well documented in galactic history.

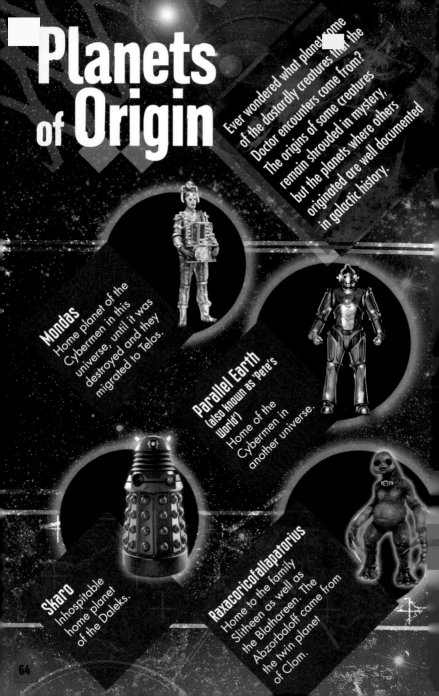

Mondas
Home planet of the Cybermen in this universe, until it was destroyed and they migrated to Telos.

Parallel Earth
(also known as 'Pete's World')
Home of the Cybermen in another universe.

Skaro
Inhospitable home planet of the Daleks.

Raxacoricofallapatorius
Home to the family Slitheen as well as the Blathereen. The Abzorbaloff came from the twin planet of Clom.

Sontar
Home planet of the Sontarans. Their enemies, the Rutan Host, are from Ruta 3.

Earth
Home world of Homo Reptilia Silurians and Sea Devils.

Mars
Where the Ice Warriors originated from.

Nestene Home World
Self-explanatory!

Rexel Planetary Configuration
Fourteen stars that are home to the Carrionites.

Silfrax Galaxy
Where the Vespiform hives are located.

Words of Wisdom

The Nestenes and Autons

"You have only seen the Autons – crude weapons with a single offensive function."
Nestene Channing

"We are the Nestenes. We have been colonising other planets for a thousand million years. Now we have come to colonise Earth."
Nestene Channing

"They're Autons – bullets can't stop them."
Third Doctor

"A Nestene is a ruthlessly aggressive intelligent alien life form... They manifest themselves as a disembodied, mutually telepathic intelligence...They have a natural affinity for plastic."
Third Doctor

"Think of it. Plastic, all over the world. Every artificial thing waiting to come alive. The shop window dummies, the phones, the wires, the cables..."
Ninth Doctor

"You're a Nestene duplicate – a lump of plastic with delusions of humanity."
Eleventh Doctor (to Rory)

Now You
See Them...

Some of the Doctor's enemies have been so small they might as well be invisible. Some of them actually are invisible. Here's a selection of just some of the invisible aliens you might see — or rather not see — as you travel round the universe.

Virus Swarm

Referred to as the 'invisible enemy', the virus swarm was actually microscopically small. Until it was accidentally grown to giant size.

Spiridons

Natives of the planet Spiridon were naturally invisible, as they could emit an anti-reflecting light wave. The Daleks enslaved them and experimented on them to discover how to become invisible themselves — with some success!

Visians

Despite their name, the Visians of the Planet Myra were invisible.

Refusians

The inhabitants of Refusis II became invisible after a giant solar flare caused a galactic accident.

Vashta Nerada

A swarm of darkness rather than strictly invisible, the Vashta Nerada are also known as Piranhas of the Air, or Shadows that eat the Flesh.

Krafayis

Appearing in a Gallifreyan fairy tale, the Krafayis are a violent race of invisible creatures. It is not known for certain whether they are all blind, or if the one encountered by the Doctor, Amy and Vincent van Gogh was injured.

Words of Wisdom

The Slitheen

"The Slitheen family —
a criminal sect from the
planet Raxacoricofallapatorius,
masquerading as a human being,
zipped inside a skin suit."
Captain Jack Harkness

"The family Slitheen
was tried in its absence many
years ago and found guilty. With
no chance of appeal."
Blon Fel Fotch
Pasameer-Day
Slitheen

"Well, it's just one family so it's not an invasion. They don't want Slitheen world... they're out to make money..."
The Ninth Doctor

"They're big old beasts, they need to fit inside big humans... That's the device around their necks — compression field — literally shrinks them down a bit. That's why there's all that gas, it's a big exchange."
The Ninth Doctor

"Calcium phosphate — organic calcium, living calcium. Creatures made out of living calcium, what else, what else? Hyphenated surname. Yes, that narrows it down to one planet: Raxacoricofallapatorius."
The Ninth Doctor

On the Run

Prisoner Zero

Imprisoned by the Atraxi, multiform Prisoner Zero was held captive in an extra-dimensional prison. But it managed to escape through a crack in the fabric of the universe that opened into Amelia Pond's bedroom. Prisoner Zero hid in Amy's house for years, until the Atraxi tracked the criminal to Earth and came to recapture it.

Morbius

Once President of the High Council of Time Lords, Morbius tried to take the Time Lords along a path of war. When this failed, he promised the Elixir of Life owned by the Sisterhood of Karn to his followers. Morbius's army was defeated and he was put on trial on Karn – where he was convicted and executed by vaporisation. But a surgeon called Mehendri Solon managed to save Morbius's brain, and set about creating a new body for his lord and master...

Slitheen

The Slitheen are a criminal family from the planet Raxacoricofallapatorius. They were arrested and tried for their crimes. Many escaped and fled, but were convicted in their absence. If any of the surviving Slitheen ever return, they will be executed.

Terileptils

A reptilian race renowned for its love of art and beauty, convicted Terileptil criminals are sent to work in the tinclavic mines on Raaga. Many of them sustain injuries and scarring as a result. A small group of Terileptils managed to escape and sought refuge on earth – releasing an enhanced variant of bubonic plague (known as the Black Death) to kill off the human population.

Look Out!

While savage alien monsters can be deadly at close quarters, even keeping well out of their way may not save you. Many alien races have a range of weapons available to them. This chart shows how dangerous some of that weaponry really is.

0

4

Auton wrist gun

Cyber-gun

Ice Warrior sonic weapon

Judoon 'peacemaker'

Dalek ray blaster

Silurian heat ray

Sontaran high-impact blaster

Sycorax sword

Words of Wisdom

The Weeping Angels

"Lonely Assassins, they were called. No one knows where they came from. They're as old as the universe, or very nearly. They've survived this long as they have the most perfect defence system ever evolved. They are quantum-locked. They don't exist when being observed. The moment they're seen by any other living creature they freeze into rock. No choice. It's a fact of their biology. In the sight of any living thing, they literally turn to stone. And you can't kill a stone."

Tenth Doctor

"This I have discerned:
That which holds the image
of Angel, becomes itself an Angel."

Book about the
Weeping Angels

"That's why they cover their eyes. They're not weeping. They can't risk looking at each other. Their greatest asset is their greatest curse – they can never be seen. The loneliest creatures in the universe."

Tenth Doctor

"But beware, for the eyes are not the windows of the soul, they are the doors. Beware what may enter there. Beware what may follow. Beware the Time of the Angels."

Book about the
Weeping Angels

"Don't blink. Don't even blink. Blink and you're dead. They are fast — faster than you can believe. Don't turn your back, don't look away, and don't blink."

Tenth Doctor

"It's not legend, it's a quantum lock. In the sight of any living creature, the Angels literally cease to exist — they're just stone. The perfect defence mechanism...Until you turn your back."

Eleventh Doctor

Chance Encounters

Throughout his long experience of travelling through time and space, the Doctor has encountered numerous aliens and monsters. Some of them he has met more than once, and others on many occasions. The chart shows which of the more persistent monsters the Doctor has encountered the most often.

- ◆ Autons and Nestenes
- ◆ Cybermen
- ◆ Daleks
- ◆ Davros
- ◆ Earth Reptile / Homo Reptilia
- ◆ Ice Warriors
- ◆ Slitheen
- ◆ Sontaran
- ◆ Weeping Angels

Back of the Neck!

However deadly and dangerous the Doctor's enemies may be, he always seems to find a weakness he can exploit. Sometimes that weakness is a flaw in their plan or even their character. But often, too, the Doctor knows of some physical weakness that he and his allies can exploit to win the day.

Cyberman

Cybermen are stronger than humans and they never tire. If they can touch you, they can kill you. But even so, remove the emotional inhibitor beneath the Cyberman's chest-plate, and the sudden rush of suppressed emotions will give it a brainstorm from which it won't recover.

Sontaran

Sontarans don't eat and drink like we do. They plug a source of energy into a socket called the probic vent at the back of their necks. They have to keep the socket relatively unprotected so they can quickly and easily 'recharge', but it's a weak point. Hit a Sontaran on the probic vent and he'll collapse. Typically, the Sontarans claim this is a strength, as it forces them to face their enemies and never turn and run away.

Dalek

The Dalek's casing protects it from almost any form of attack. The weakest point is the eyestalk at the top of the dome. But even that is incredibly resilient. You would need some pretty heavy weaponry, like bastic bullets, to take it off and blind a Dalek.

Ice Warrior

As their nickname implies, the original natives of Mars like the cold. Turn the temperature up too much, and an Ice Warrior will keel over from heat exhaustion. At really high temperatures, it is said that they melt away completely.

Slitheen

Made of living calcium, the Slitheen are vulnerable to acid, which destroys their alkaline bodies. Mix up a potion of vinegar and pickles, and throw it over an attacking Slitheen – then you're in business.

Myths and Legends

Sometimes, the facts get blurred and become fiction. There are myths and legends on many planets about creatures that are actually real — and the facts are often stranger than fiction.

◇◇◇

The Loch Ness Monster

The Fourth Doctor discovered that the legendary Loch Ness Monster was actually an armoured cyborg creature, brought to Earth as an embryo by a group of Zygons when their spaceship crashed into the Loch. But after the Doctor defeated the Zygons, and the Skarasen was free of their control, it returned to its home — Loch Ness.

The Sixth Doctor also encountered an alien dictator called the Borad. Hideously mutated after an experiment went wrong, the Borad fell through a Timelash and also ended up in Loch Ness. So perhaps there are actually two monsters in the Loch...

Egyptian Mummies

The walking mummies that the Fourth Doctor and Sarah Jane Smith came up against were actually Osiran Service Robots. They were wrapped in bandages infused with chemicals to stop the robots from corrosion, and were controlled by the imprisoned Osiran criminal Sutekh.

Ghosts

There are many explanations for the apparitions people call ghosts. Sometimes they are manifestations brought about by a time rift. Sometimes they are time travellers, appearing in one era before fading back to their own. In Victorian Cardiff, the Ninth Doctor and Rose encountered a race of ethereal creatures called the Gelth who could possess dead bodies and planned to take over the human race...

The Beast

Imprisoned before the start of time on Krop Tor, the hideous Beast might be the source of legendary devil-like creatures across the universe. The Tenth Doctor speculated that the devil-legends of Earth, Draconia, Vel Consadine, Damos, and even the Kaled God of War might stem originally from the Beast.

Time and Again . . .

The Time Lords were the undisputed guardians of time and space.
But they were not the only race to develop some form of time travel
technology. Only the Daleks rival the Time Lords' technology, but
others have managed to travel in time one way or another — like the
race that built the time ship that was stranded above Craig Owens' flat
in Aickman Road. Others have a relationship with time that is still not
fully understood — like the Trickster and his Brigade.

Daleks

Dalek temporal technology has developed
and improved. They used to be able to
travel through time only between fixed
points in each era, using unreliable
devices. From this they developed
the capability of creating time
corridors from one era to another.
Finally they managed to achieve full
time technology. This enabled them
to send an assassination squad after the
TARDIS to try to kill the Doctor. Later, of
course, the Daleks fought the Time Lords in the
Great Time War.

Humans

Many humans have experimen
with time travel — with limited
success. Professor Whitaker
developed a 'time scoop' that
could bring dinosaurs into the
heart of modern day London.
The Russian Aaron Blinovitch
is perhaps the most famous
temporal scientist.

Pyroviles

The Pyroviles did not actually possess the ability to travel in time. Their appearance in ancient Pompeii was a side effect of their planet being 'stolen' by the Daleks.

Sontarans

The Sontarans can use osmic projection to achieve a low degree of time travel. A stranded Sontaran – Commander Linx – used this unreliable and risky process to kidnap scientists from the twentieth century to help him repair his spaceship which had crashed on Earth in medieval times.

Weeping Angels

The so-called Weeping Angels have a special relationship with time. This affinity enables them to send people back into the distant past, and harvest the temporal energy this creates as the potential of their futures lives is destroyed. The Angels themselves cannot travel in time as such.

Friend
or Foe?

Before their true nature and intentions are revealed, the most dastardly alien creature can seem friendly, or at least not outright hostile. When the First Doctor and his companions met the Daleks for the first time, they had no idea they were pitiless, evil creatures and even believed they might provide food and supplies for their mortal enemies, the Thals. But sometimes, the monsters have deliberately disguised their true nature and pretended to be friendly. Beware of aliens bearing gifts!

Daleks

The Daleks are cunning and clever enough to pretend to be friendly and helpful if it furthers their plans. On the colony Vulcan, a group of Daleks pretended to be helpful robots ready to se████ umans. Stranded without t██████ their weapons on the planet Exxilon, the Daleks even seemed willing to enter into an alliance with the Doctor – but broke the truce as soon as they had fitted themselves with new machine gun weapons. During the Second World War, two Daleks pretended they were new Ironside weapons invented by Professor Bracewell. But once again this was all part of a cunning and deadly plan...

Cybermen (aka the Army of Ghosts)

People thought the Cybermen from a parallel world that partially materialised in our own world were ghosts. They thought they must be dead relatives and friends come back to rejoin the living. The Cybermen let this misconception go unchallenged until they were ready to materialise fully, and invade.

Axons

The Axons offered the human race an amazing material called Axonite which seemed to solve the problems of famine and energy creation. But in fact, the Axons and the Axonite itself were all part of a galactic parasite called Axos. Once they had spread Axonite through the world, the Axons planned to use it to drain Earth's energy.

Gelth

The Gelth were ethereal, bodiless creatures that pretended to need help. For a while, even the Doctor was taken in. But then he realised the Gelth wanted to possess the bodies of everyone on Earth.

Plasmavore

The Plasmavore that hid from the Judoon at the Royal Hope Hospital in London pretended to be a harmless old lady called Florence. In fact, she was a blood-sucking vampire who had already murdered the Child Princess of Padrivole Regency Nine.

87

Attack of the Earthlings

Not all the monsters that have endangered life on our planet have come from outer space. Some of them have been 'home-grown' – actually originating on Earth. We've had our share of villainous scientists and ruthless dictators, but we've been home to some unpleasant monsters too.

Giant Maggots

Global Chemicals secretly disposed of toxic waste from its oil refining process in an abandoned coal mine in Wales. Maggots contaminated by the waste grew to giant size and burrowed out of the mine. Their bite was fatal and the Doctor and UNIT had to destroy them before they grew into flies and spread across the world.

Cybermen

Not quite of our Earth, the Cybermen originally evolved both on Earth's twin planet Mondas – which drifted away through space until its return in 1986 – and also on a parallel version of Earth where they were developed by John Lumic.

The Primords

Infected by a viscous green fluid that bubbled up a drilling shaft, scientists and soldiers at the Inferno Project were transformed into primordial humanoid monsters intent on killing.

STAHLMANN

Silurians and Sea Devils

These intelligent reptiles of prehistoric Earth went into hibernation millions of years ago to avoid destruction, but they have awoken and sought to reclaim the planet they believe to be their own on several occasions.

Words of Wisdom

The Doctor

"He never raised his voice. That was the worst thing – the fury of the Time Lord. And then we discovered why. Why this Doctor, who had fought with gods and demons, why he'd run away from us and hidden. He was being kind."

Son of Mine

"You are the Doctor. You will be deleted."

Cyberman

"You are the Doctor. You are an enemy of the Daleks. You will be exterminated!"

Dalek

"The man who abhors violence, never carrying a gun. But, this is the truth, Doctor – you take ordinary people and you fashion them into weapons. Behold your Children of Time, transformed into murderers."

Davros

"There was a goblin, or a trickster. Or a warrior. A nameless, terrible thing, soaked in the blood of a billion galaxies – the most feared being in all the cosmos. And nothing could stop it or hold it, or reason with it. One day it would just drop out of the sky and tear down your world."

The Myth of the Pandorica

"If you had any more tawdry quirks, you could open a tawdry quirk shop. The madcap vehicle, the cockamamie hair, the clothes designed by a first-year fashion student. I'm surprised you haven't got a little purple space dog, just to ram home what an intergalactic wag you are."

The Dream Lord

Part Creature,
Part Machine

Things are not always as they appear. A Cyberman might look like a robot, but it is partly organic. Equally, the Loch Ness Monster might look like a huge dinosaur, but it's actually an armoured cyborg, with mechanical components and implants, brought to Earth by the Zygons...

Cybermen

When Amy found the head of a Cyberman hidden in the vault under Stonehenge, she thought it was part of a robot. But when the head snapped open to reveal the remains of a human skull inside, she realised that the Cybermen are actually cyborgs – people augmented by mechanical and computer components. Amy was lucky to escape being cybernised herself!

Davros

Wizened and ancient, the Kaled scientist Davros is kept alive by the mechanical life support facilities of his special wheelchair. It enhances his hearing and his vision, as well as providing a means of transport. Davros later adapted this same technology to create his 'Mark 3 Travel Machine' to house the mutated creatures he knew his race would become – the Daleks.

Daleks

When people first encounter a Dalek, they assume it is a robot. But inside the Dalek 'shell' is the Dalek Creature – a hideously mutated being dependent on radiation to survive. The Dalek casing is a travel machine for the monstrous creature inside, which hates all other life forms and wants to see them exterminated.

Toclafane

Like flying metal footballs, with inbuilt armaments, the Toclafane seem to be entirely mechanical. But inside each is the desiccated remains of one of the very last human beings from the far future.

Bannakaffalatta

A member of the Zocci race, Bannakaffalatta was a passenger on the doomed starship *Titanic*. He was part-cyborg and died when he used his robotic components to release an electromagnetic pulse that temporarily disabled the Host robots that were attacking the passengers.

93

Chap With Wings...

One of the most famous orders given by Brigadier Lethbridge-Stewart during his time as commander of the UK contingent of UNIT was: "Chap with wings — five rounds rapid." But the five bullets had no effect on Bok, the grotesque statue animated by the Master... Over the years, UNIT has fought against many monstrous threats, as well as the Doctor's old enemy the Master, and saved Earth from invasion many times. Here are just some of the monsters listed in the UNIT files.

AUTONS

PRIMORDS

STAHLMANN

DALEKS

KRAALS

SONTARANS

SILURIANS

AZAL, last of the Daemons

OGRONS

ZYGONS

CYBERMEN

KRYNOID

AXONS

95

Did You Know...
About the Cybermen?

You might think you know everything there is to know about the Cybermen, but did you know...?

The design of the Cybermen has changed over the years as they 'evolve' and discover better and more efficient ways of enhancing themselves.

The Cybermen were once so close to extinction that they retreated to frozen tombs on their home planet of Telos, waiting to be found by human archaeologists who could then be turned into a new race of Cybermen.

Cybermats are small rodent-like mechanical creatures created by the Cybermen. They are cybernised animals.

In the Cyberwars, the human race discovered that Cybermen were susceptible to gold, which could clog up their breathing apparatus, and invented 'glitter gun' to use against Cybermen.

The most important Cyberman is the Cyber Controller. There have been several Cyber Controllers over the years.

The Cybermen evolved both on a parallel version of Earth where they were created by John Lumic, and in our own universe on Earth's long-lost twin planet, Mondas.

The Second Doctor faced – and defeated – the Cybermen more than any other monster, even the Daleks.

Few races are more deadly and dangerous than the Cybermen, though they have been defeated by humanity, Raton Warrior Robots, and the Daleks.

Cybershades are part organic, part cybernetic creatures. Created from local materials and available technology, the Cybermen used them in Victorian London, as they are more agile but less noticeable than ordinary Cybermen.

Reasons for
Invading
Earth

Many monstrous creatures have tried to invade Earth over the millennia. Some have been after our minerals and natural resources, others have sought to enslave the human race. Sometimes Earth has been deemed strategically important in a conflict fought out among distant stars, and sometimes the aggression is purely malevolent... This chart shows most of the more usual reasons for attempted invasion — as well as a few of the more bizarre.

To enslave the human race

To use the human race itself as a resource

As part of a scientific experiment

To plunder Earth's natural resources

To plunder the resources created by the human race

To make Earth their own planet

To reclaim the planet for its 'rightful' owners

To use Earth as a cloning or breeding planet

To use Earth as a strategic military base

To help Earth's plants destroy all animal life

To replace Earth's core with a guidance system and turn it into a spaceship

To exterminate all humans

You might think you know everything there is to know about the Sycorax, but did you know...?

Sycorax robes are often decorated with trophies taken from enemies killed in battle.

Although they are warriors, the Sycorax would rather win a battle by deception than by force of arms.

The Sycorax are an honourable race – a Sycorax leader will rarely refuse the offer of a challenge or trial by combat.

Sycorax spaceships are made from rock.

Captives are often held prisoner in metal cages hung inside the cavernous interior of a Sycorax spaceship, and left to die.

The Sycorax speak a language called Sycoraxic.

Sycorax technology relies not just on conventional science but also on more arcane practices such as 'blood control'.

The
Regeneration
Game

The Doctor has regenerated many times during his long life. According to some legends, a Time Lord can only regenerate twelve times, but others say the limit is 507. Still more suggest that there is actually no limit... Whatever the truth, there are many questions that remain unanswered. Was the old man we think of as the First Doctor really the Doctor's first incarnation? Or were there other Doctors even before that?

Cybermen

The First Doctor regenerated after defeating the Cybermen, though in fact he had been frail for some time. It is likely that his body just wore out from old age, but battling against the Cybermen for the first time can't have helped.

Time Lords

More than any other race, it is the Time Lords that have been responsible for making the Doctor regenerate. After they put him on trial for interfering in the affairs of other worlds and times, the Time Lords changed the Second Doctor's appearance and exiled his third incarnation to twentieth century Earth. The Fourth Doctor regenerated after the rogue Time Lord, the Master, engineered his fall from a radio telescope. The Tenth Doctor regenerated after saving Wilfred Mott following his battle against the Time Lords led by Rassilon.

Daleks

The Daleks were instrumental in the Doctor regenerating into his tenth incarnation, as it was because of them that Rose Tyler absorbed the energy of the Time Vortex from the TARDIS. The Doctor then took it from her, prompting his regeneration. Being shot by a Dalek also caused the Tenth Doctor to regenerate – into the same body once more. The regeneration of the Eighth Doctor into his Ninth incarnation is shrouded in mystery, but may have come about during the Great Time War between the Time Lords and the Daleks.

Giant Spectrox Bat

The Fifth Doctor was forced to regenerate after contracting spectrox toxaemia from a nest of one of the bats on Androzani Minor.

The Great One

The Third Doctor's body was destroyed by radiation he absorbed from the crystal lattice that formed the cave of the Great One – a huge spider on the planet Metabelis Three.

Did You Know...
About the Silurians?

You might think you know everything there is to know about the Silurians, but did you know…?

'Silurian' is a period of prehistory. The man who first discovered the Silurians thought they originated in this time period, but he was wrong.

The Silurians are also known as Earth Reptiles, Homo Reptilia, or sometimes Eocenes (after another period of prehistory – again not the one from which they come).

There are many different tribes and types of Silurians, quite distinct from each other. One type of Silurian has a third eye in their forehead, which they can use to burn through rock.

Silurian technology is far more advanced, but very different, to our own.

The Silurians were once the dominant intelligent life form on Earth. But they went into deep hibernation chambers to escape the catastrophe they thought would be caused by the collision of a huge asteroid with Earth. But the catastrophe never happened, so the Silurians were never woken. The asteroid went into orbit around Earth instead – and became the moon.

The Silurians still see humans as upstart apes.

The aquatic, underwater Silurians encountered by the Third and Fifth Doctors were nicknamed 'Sea Devils'.

The Silurians have the ability to control other larger prehistoric animals like certain dinosaurs and the terrifying Myrka – which can kill with an electric charge.

Uneasy Allies – Master and Servants

The Doctor's arch-enemy the Master has often worked with alien creatures and other villains in his schemes to create universal chaos. Often, he has betrayed his allies – and was once even executed by the Daleks for his crimes. These are some of the creatures the Master has worked with over the millennia.

Axons – in fact, the alien parasite Axos captured the Master and forced him to take them to Earth. As soon as he could he betrayed Axos and escaped.

Daemons – the Master sought to succeed the last of the Daemons, Azal, as ruler of Earth.

Daleks – the Master was actually working for the Daleks when he tried to provoke war between Earth and Draconia.

Sea Devils – even though he was in prison at the time, the Master helped the Sea Devils in their bid to reclaim 'their' planet from the human race.

Kronos the Chronovore – the Master tried to tame and control this terrifying creature. He failed, and was lucky to escape with his life.

The Time Lords – the Master unwittingly and unwillingly helped the Time Lords in their attempt to survive the terrible Time War against the Daleks.

Nestenes and Autons – the Master helped them establish a bridgehead on Earth. He betrayed them when captured by UNIT.

Toclafane – the Master brought the Toclafane back through time from the far future to help him conquer Earth.

Ogrons – the Master used the Ogrons as his henchmen in his plan to set the empires of Earth and Draconia at war.

From the
Depths

Most of the enemies the Doctor has fought have been firmly based on land – be it on Earth, another planet or even out in deep space. But he has also faced creatures that live for some of the time in water. Here are various aquatic creatures the Doctor has encountered on his travels.

Fish

When he visited Sardicktown, the Doctor found an environment where fish could live in the clouds. Occasionally, they descended to the surface of the planet in fog and mist. Not much fun if you meet a shark in your bedroom!

Fish People

The deluded Professor Zaroff turned some of the citizens of the underwater city Atlantis into 'fish people', who were able to breathe underwater and could harvest food for the city.

The Flood

On Mars, the Doctor faced a terrifying life form that lived in water and possessed anyone who came into contact with that water.

Hath

The Doctor managed to broker a peace between the warring humans and Hath on the colony planet Messaline. The Hath were aquatic creatures, breathing oxygenated liquid through a special respirator when on land.

Saturnynes

Although they disguised themselves as humans, the Saturnynes who came to Venice were a form of giant carnivorous fish.

Sea Devils

Nicknamed 'Sea Devils', the underwater 'cousins' of the Silurians tried to reclaim Earth, but were defeated by the Doctor with the help of the Royal Navy.

Double Trouble

It's a brave person or alien that tries to impersonate the Doctor, but some have attempted it over the years. As well as accidental doubles for the Doctor, like the Abbot of Amboise, who happened to look like the First Doctor, or the misguided world leader Salamander, who was very similar to the Second Doctor, there have been some deliberate Doctor-copies...

The Daleks

Of course, the Doctor doesn't look anything like a Dalek, but his greatest enemies once created a robot double of the First Doctor to trick his companions.

Meglos

A form of intelligent xerophyte, the last Zolfa-Thuran changed his form to copy the Fourth Doctor. But the process involved the unwilling use of a kidnapped human, and when Meglos's concentration lapsed, the body reverted to part-cactus form, with spikes and green skin...

Xoanon

The Doctor inadvertently made a copy of his brain patterns when he repaired the main computer on the Mordee Expedition. He forgot to wipe his personality from the computer's memory, and it developed into an insane version of the Fourth Doctor that was worshipped as a god by the tribes of Tesh and Sevateem.

Cessair of Diplos

The criminal Cessair of Diplos used the power of a segment of the Key to Time to impersonate the Fourth Doctor and lure Romana over the edge of a cliff.

Omega

To escape from the universe of anti-matter, renegade Time Lord scientist Omega stole a copy of the Doctor's bio-data. From this he created a copy of the Fifth Doctor. But the copy was unstable, and Omega was destroyed.

Cassandra

Cassandra didn't actually copy the Doctor's body, but she did manage to take over his own body for a while – much to Rose's irritation.

Did You Know...

About the Weeping Angels?

You might think you know everything there is to know about the Weeping Angels, but did you know…?

The real name of the Weeping Angels is the Lonely Assassins.

They are thought to be as old as the universe itself.

It isn't just the statues themselves you have to watch out for – even an image or recording of a Weeping Angel can be dangerous.

The Weeping Angels can't control the defensive mechanism that turns them to stone if they are being watched – that's why they often cover their eyes with their hands, so that they don't accidentally look at each other.

While they are nicknamed 'Weeping Angels', the Lonely Assassins can take any form – so any statue could actually be one of them, ready to attack as soon as you look away...

The Best Laid Plans

Invading a planet like Earth is never a straightforward proposition, but some attempted invasions have been more complicated than others. These diagrams show several invasion plans — none of which went entirely as they should have done, thanks to the intervention of the Doctor.

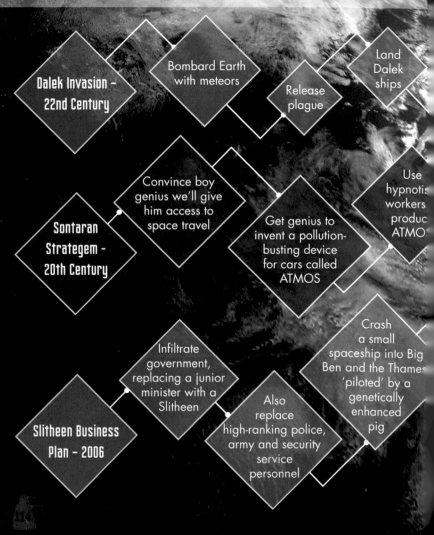

Dalek Invasion – 22nd Century

Bombard Earth with meteors

Release plague

Land Dalek ships

Sontaran Strategem – 20th Century

Convince boy genius we'll give him access to space travel

Get genius to invent a pollution-busting device for cars called ATMOS

Use hypnotised workers to produce ATMOS

Slitheen Business Plan – 2006

Infiltrate government, replacing a junior minister with a Slitheen

Also replace high-ranking police, army and security service personnel

Crash a small spaceship into Big Ben and the Thames 'piloted' by a genetically enhanced pig

Turn some people into Robomen. Make others work in a mine in Bedfordshire

Use explosive capsule to blow out Earth's molten core

Replace Earth's core with a guidance system and engines so the planet becomes a giant spaceship

Dig down to the centre of the Earth

Clone members of UNIT in case they try to fight back

Make ATMOS so successful that it is fitted to all cars. Include a satellite navigation system that can be used to kill anyone who causes problems

Use ATMOS to pump atmosphere full of lethal chemicals that turn Earth into a Sontaran Clone World

Get the UN to release nuclear weapons for use

Get all other Slitheen into Downing Street

Use Earth's own nuclear weapons to destroy the plan

Kill the PM and ensure other Cabinet members are unavailable so that junior Slitheen minister is in charge

Persuade the people that there's an alien invasion underway

Sell the resulting waste to the highest bidders

Did You Know...
About the Sontarans

You might think you know everything there is to know about the Sontarans, but did you know...?

The Sontarans have been at war with the Rutan host for thousands of years.

The Sontarans once invaded Gallifrey, but were defeated by the Doctor – who was then President of the Time Lords.

Using osmic projection, Sontarans have limited time travel capability.

Sontarans don't eat food, they recharge from pure energy that they take in through the probic vent at the back of their neck.

They don't just clone themselves, the Sontarans can produce clone copies of other species too, which they then control. They once cloned the Doctor's friend, Martha.

The Sontaran home planet Sontar has very high gravity, which is why the Sontarans evolved to be so physically strong and powerful.

A cloned race, the Sontarans can produce a million new warriors every three minutes.

Evolution of the Daleks

Over the centuries since they were first created by Davros, the design of the Daleks' casings has changed and improved as they discover and add new features and technology.

Original Design
The original Daleks, which the First Doctor encountered in their city on Skaro, were much the same as the Daleks of today. But they were smaller, and all were mainly metallic silver in colour.

Dalek Invasion of Earth
The Daleks that invaded Earth in the 22nd century had enlarged base sections and received energy transmissions through a circular dish on their backs.

Return of the Dalek

The Ninth Doctor was devastated to discover that the Daleks had survived the Time War in a new, improved form...

Power Slats

Power slats round the mid-section of the Dalek collect and store energy. The very first Daleks could only travel on special metal floors that supplied static electricity to power their casings. The very latest Daleks have reverted to more simple bands in this section.

Attachments

The multi-purpose Dalek sucker arm can be replaced with a variety of specialist tools, from metal-cutters to preceptor detection devices.

Latest Design

The new race of Dalek created by the progenitor device is larger than previous Daleks, with a simplified mid-section.

You might think you know everything there is to know about the Slitheen, but did you know...?

'Slitheen' is not the name of their race. They are a family from the planet Raxacoricofallapatorius, and Slitheen is their surname.

The Slitheen, like all other Raxacoricofallapatorians, are made of calcium.

The Slitheen have a highly-sensitive sense of smell, which they use when hunting their prey.

Slitheen hatch from eggs.

An endangered female Slitheen can fire a poison dart from her claw.

The Slitheen were once powerful on their planet, but they were exposed and shamed as criminals.

The Slitheen can squeeze themselves down into human body suits – so beware, as your best friend or favourite teacher might actually be a Slitheen!

Defeats of the Sontarans

The Doctor has encountered the warlike Sontarans on several occasions, and each time he has defeated them. Here's how:

The Third Doctor found that scientists were being kidnapped from the twentieth century and taken back to medieval times by Sontaran Commander Linx, who needed their help to repair his crashed spaceship. Linx spurned the Doctor's offers of help, instead arming local warlord Irongron with rifles and an armoured robot knight. Linx managed to repair his ship, but was killed by an arrow from the Doctor's friend, Hal the archer.

On the abandoned Earth of the far future, the Fourth Doctor found Field Major Styre conducting experiments on captured humans. The Doctor and his friends sabotaged Styre's spaceship, so that when he tried to re-energize himself he was killed.

The Doctor led Time Lord resistance against the Sontarans who invaded Gallifrey – killing their Commander Stor with a powerful Demat Gun.

The Sontarans who kidnapped the Second Doctor from Space Station Camera were betrayed and killed by their former allies, the Androgums. The Second Doctor was rescued by the Sixth Doctor.

The Sontaran stratagem to turn Earth into a clone world was defeated when the Doctor set an atmospheric converter to destroy their ship.

Skin Deep . . .

The life forms of the universe are infinitely variable. As well as the most evil creatures imaginable, most life forms are friendly and hospitable. And you can't tell from its appearance whether an alien is hostile or amicable. Just as you should be wary of beautiful-looking creatures – like the Movellans and the Axons – that might turn out to be hostile, so you also need to be careful not to assume an ugly, monstrous-looking alien means you harm. It might just want to be loved. Here are some aliens who might not seem attractive to humans, but have good intentions nonetheless.

Cryons

Original inhabitants of the planet Telos before it was colonised by the Cybermen.

Draconians

An ancient and noble race steeped in honour. For a while the empires of Earth and Draconia were at war, but peace finally prevailed.

Exxilon Rebels

The Exxilons were enslaved by the Daleks, but some rebels held out and helped the Doctor and an Earth Marine Space Corps mission.

Foamasi

While some of the reptilian Foamasi are part of a criminal organisation called the West Lodge, the race is generally law-abiding.

Hath

Despite occasional disagreements, humans and Hath have worked together in harmony to redevelop worlds for colonisation by both races.

Judoon

They might look fierce and they tolerate no objections or interference, but the Judoon are dedicated to upholding the rule of law. They are even used for security duties by the powerful Shadow Proclamation.

Ood

The Ood were used as servants – almost as slaves – for many years. Deferential and subservient, they are now a free race thanks to the Doctor's intervention.

Skin Deep . . .
...Continued

Rills

Revolting-looking tusked porcine creatures that live in ammonia fumes, the Rills and their robots the Chumbleys mean no harm.

Silurians

While they are determined to reclaim 'their' planet, the Earth Reptiles have, on several occasions, indicated that they might be able to live in peace with humanity on Earth.

and Sea Devils

Space Pig

Not actually an alien, but a real farmyard pig that had been genetically enhanced by the Slitheen as part of a ruse to invade Earth.

Star Whale

The Star Whale that came to Earth and was harnessed as a drive force for *Starship UK* was actually trying to help – and happy to continue to help by powering the spaceship.

Tharils

Time sensitive leonine mesomorphs, the Tharils once had a great, oppressive empire. After the people they had enslaved rose up and destroyed them using Gundan Robots, the Tharils themselves were enslaved.

Tythonians

Giant, green blobs that feed on plant matter, the Tythonians are technically advanced and able to 'spin' their own egg-like spaceships.

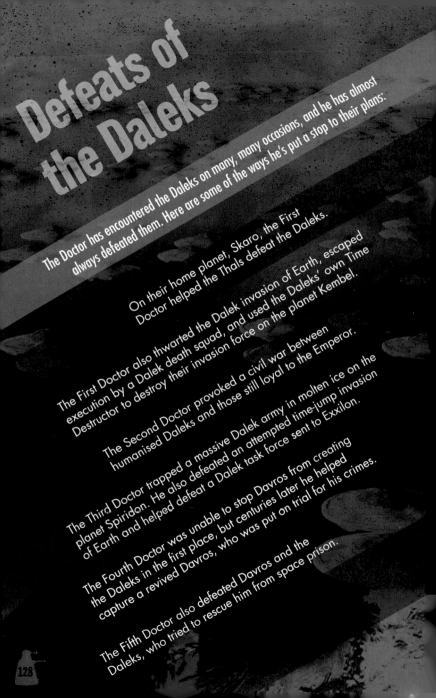

Defeats of the Daleks

The Doctor has encountered the Daleks on many, many occasions, and he has almost always defeated them. Here are some of the ways he's put a stop to their plans:

On their home planet, Skaro, the First Doctor helped the Thals defeat the Daleks.

The First Doctor also thwarted the Dalek invasion of Earth, escaped execution by a Dalek death squad, and used the Daleks' own Time Destructor to destroy their invasion force on the planet Kembel.

The Second Doctor provoked a civil war between humanised Daleks and those still loyal to the Emperor.

The Third Doctor trapped a massive Dalek army in molten ice on the planet Spiridon. He also defeated an attempted time-jump invasion of Earth and helped defeat a Dalek task force sent to Exxilon.

The Fourth Doctor was unable to stop Davros from creating the Daleks in the first place, but centuries later he helped capture a revived Davros, who was put on trial for his crimes.

The Fifth Doctor also defeated Davros and the Daleks, who tried to rescue him from space prison.

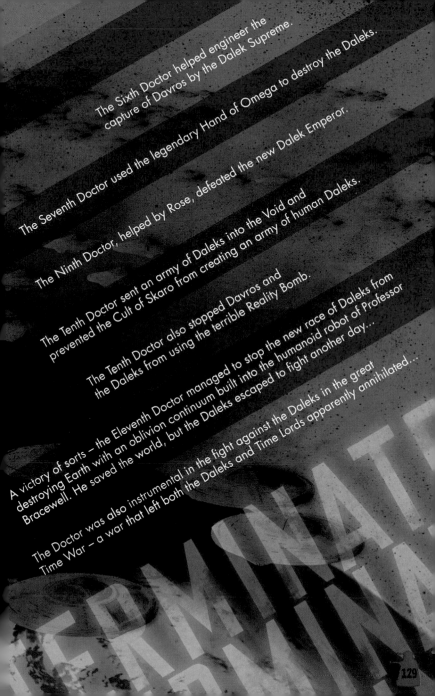

The Sixth Doctor helped engineer the capture of Davros by the Dalek Supreme.

The Seventh Doctor used the legendary Hand of Omega to destroy the Daleks.

The Ninth Doctor, helped by Rose, defeated the new Dalek Emperor.

The Tenth Doctor sent an army of Daleks into the Void and prevented the Cult of Skaro from creating an army of human Daleks.

The Tenth Doctor also stopped Davros and the Daleks from using the terrible Reality Bomb.

A victory of sorts – the Eleventh Doctor managed to stop the new race of Daleks from destroying Earth with an oblivion continuum built into the humanoid robot of Professor Bracewell. He saved the world, but the Daleks escaped to fight another day…

The Doctor was also instrumental in the fight against the Daleks in the great Time War – a war that left both the Daleks and Time Lords apparently annihilated…

Did You Know...
About the Judoon?

You might think you know everything there is to know about the Judoon, but did you know...?

The Judoon are freelance law-enforcers. Other species employ them as policemen.

The fabled Shadow Proclamation use Judoon for their security forces.

The Judoon can only enforce Galactic Law when specifically invited to do so, or on neutral territory.

Anyone opposing the Judoon is automatically found guilty and may be executed on the spot.

Judoon technology allows them to scan life forms and discover what species they are.

The Judoon speak their own guttural language — but their technology translates it into any other language necessary.

The Judoon sometimes use an H_2O scoop. They harness the inert power of hydrogen to transport people, or even whole buildings, to neutral space, where the Judoon can enforce the law.

Alien Alliances

Not all hostile alien races work alone. And sometimes even powerful races like the Daleks have found it useful or necessary to enter into an alliance with other creatures. But these alliances are often uneasy and rarely last. Here are a few notable examples of monstrous cooperation.

Daleks and Ogrons

An unequal alliance, the Daleks use the Ogrons as 'guard dogs' on planets they have conquered when they don't need a large Dalek presence to keep control. The Master also used the Ogrons, but was himself working for the Daleks.

United Galactic Headquarters

An alliance of various alien races brought together by the Daleks on the planet Kembel, to create an army to destroy the Earth Empire. Mavic Chen, the treacherous Guardian of the Solar System also joined them. The alliance was dissolved when the Daleks exterminated all other members – including Chen.

The Galactic Federation

Actually a peaceful organisation dedicated to sharing resources and knowledge as well as free trade, though it went to war with Galaxy Five. The Federation included (amongst others) humans, the inhabitants of the planet Peladon, the 'people' of Alpha Centauri, of Arcturus, and of Vega Nexos, and the Ice Warriors.

Sontarans and Vardans

The Vardans, creatures that can travel along any broadcast wavelength, formed the spearhead of the Sontaran invasion of Gallifrey.

The Pandorica Alliance

The full extent of the alliance put together to create the Pandorica and imprison the Doctor inside it is still not known. But it certainly included the Daleks, Cybermen, Nestene Consciousness, Sontarans, Sycorax, Earth Reptiles, Slitheen, Judoon, Drahvins, Blowfish aliens, Chelonians, Hoix, Roboforms, Uvodni, Weevils, Zygons, and Atraxi.

Your Anti-Monster Kit

You never know when a hideous alien monster might be waiting for you just round the next corner. So be prepared, have an anti-alien monster kit ready and waiting. Of course, it's impossible to predict which monsters you might have to defend yourself against. And against some monsters, there is no defence. But think about keeping some of the following handy:

Vinegar and Pickled Onions — to dissolve a Slitheen's calcium skin.

Bastic Bullets — capable of damaging a Dalek's eyestalk

Silver Bullets — defence against werewolves (mistletoe also useful)

High-energy Ultra High Frequency (UHF) transmitter —
can block Nestene instructions to Autons

Phial of Krillitane Oil — the Krillitane are allergic to their own oil

Small Hammer — suitable for bashing a Sontaran's probic vent

Mirror — to reflect sunlight at vampires, moonlight
at werewolves, or reflect an invisible Krafayis

Torch — to see what you are facing, and also to check for 'extra' shadows
caused by the Vashta Nerada

Evolution of
The Cybermen

Over the centuries since they were first created, the Cybermen have changed and refined their design as they discover or scavenge new technology.

Original Design

The Cybermen the First Doctor encountered, who came from Earth's twin planet Mondas, were primitive by modern standards. Their faces were made of a blank, cloth-like material and the 'handles' either side of the head supported a lamp above the skull. The chest units were large and cumbersome, and the Cybermen's hands were still completely human.

Entombed Cybermen

The Cybermen who emerged from their ice tombs on the planet Telos – like those who attacked the Moonbase in 2070 – were much closer to modern Cyber design. They had metal helmets that covered their heads, with the 'handles' and lamp incorporated into them. The chest units, while still bulky, were less cumbersome. Similar, but 'sleeker' Cybermen attacked Station 3 (also known as the Wheel in Space).

Enlarged Helmet Design

The Cybermen who hid in the London sewers and attacked with the help of International Electromatics had more compact chest units, but enlarged heads. Similar helmet design continued into the Cyberwars, although later Cybermen from this era, and those who tried to obtain the so-called Silver Nemesis statue, were of a more refined design.

Modern Cybermen

The Cybermen designed by John Lumic and his scientists at Cybus Industries combined the best attributes of the Cybermen from our own universe. They have no chest unit as such, their bodies being encased in plated armour and their chests embossed with the Cybus logo.

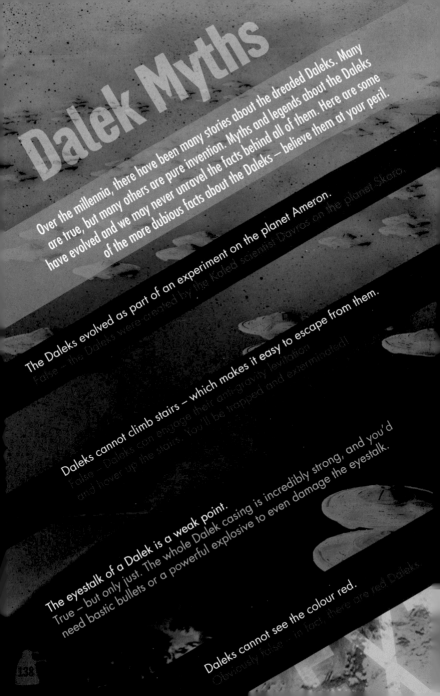

Dalek Myths

Over the millennia, there have been many stories about the dreaded Daleks. Many are true, but many others are pure invention. Myths and legends about the Daleks have evolved and we may never unravel the facts behind all of them. Here are some of the more dubious facts about the Daleks – believe them at your peril.

The Daleks evolved as part of an experiment on the planet Ameron.
False – the Daleks were created by the Kaled scientist Davros on the planet Skaro.

Daleks cannot climb stairs – which makes it easy to escape from them.
False – Daleks can engage their anti-gravity levitation and hover up the stairs. You'll be trapped and exterminated!

The eyestalk of a Dalek is a weak point.
True – but only just. The whole Dalek casing is incredibly strong, and you'd need bastic bullets or a powerful explosive to even damage the eyestalk.

Daleks cannot see the colour red.
Obviously false – in fact, there are red Daleks.

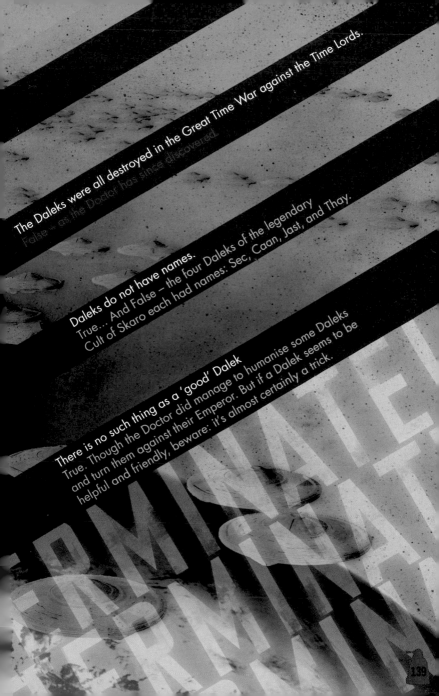

The Daleks were all destroyed in the Great Time War against the Time Lords.
False – as the Doctor has since discovered.

Daleks do not have names.
True... And False – the four Daleks of the legendary Cult of Skaro each had names: Sec, Caan, Jast, and Thay.

There is no such thing as a 'good' Dalek
True. Though the Doctor did manage to humanise some Daleks and turn them against their Emperor. But if a Dalek seems to be helpful and friendly, beware: it's almost certainly a trick.

Ranks of
The Cybermen

The command structure of the Cyber Race has always been unclear. The Cybermen don't tend to advertise their different ranks and sometimes they are indistinguishable in physical appearance. But here is what we do know:

Cyberman

Most Cybermen are just Cybermen, equal and without specific rank. The rank and file Cybermen may be allotted different tasks, but any Cyberman is equally capable of taking on any role or task it is given.

Cyber Lieutenant

The lowest rank of Cyberman 'officer' is the Cyber Lieutenant. He usually reports to a Cyberleader and is responsible for making sure that Cyberleader's orders are carried out.

Cyber Leader

Not all Cyberleaders have a Cyber Lieutenant reporting to them. Also, while some Cyberleaders are distinguished from their minions by black head markings, this is not always the case.

Other Cyber creatures

Cybermat

The Cybermat is a rodent-like cybernetic creature, possibly converted from (or using the brain of) a small animal such as a rat or a cat. Cybermats perform limited – but deadly – functions.

Cyber Android

The Cybermen occasionally use blank, featureless androids programmed for a specific task. Because of their appearance, these androids are sometimes referred to as Silhouettes.

Cybershade

A large, dark, shaggy creature enhanced with Cyber head and hands, the Cybershade is more animal than Cyberman. Cybershades are agile, but deadly, and often used for reconnaissance.

Cyber King

The so-called CyberKing is actually a Dreadnought-class Cybership, complete with a Cyber Production/Conversion Factory on-board. Since the ship takes the form of a giant Cyber figure, it is assumed to have an intelligence of its own, but there is no evidence for this.

Cyber Controller

The highest rank is the Cyber Controller. There is only one Controller at any given time, in overall charge of all Cyber operations. The Cyber Controller's design has changed through the generations, but generally he has an enlarged helmet housing a super-enhanced brain.

Davros

A Kaled scientist from the planet Skaro, Davros found a way for his race to survive the terrible thousand-year war they fought against the Thals. He created a travel machine and life support system for the creature he knew his people would eventually mutate into – their bodies poisoned by the chemical, biological, and radioactive weapons used in the war. He called this machine the 'Dalek', and he made genetic changes to the Kaled mutants, so that they would be without feeling or pity, and would hate all other life forms with a vengeance.

Electronic eye

Speech is enhanced

Single cybernetic hand

Control systems for life support, communication, etc

Wheelchair may have been the prototype design for the base of the Dalek

143

Ranks of the Daleks

The command structure of the Daleks has varied through time. We know they are traditionally ruled by an Emperor who presides over a Supreme Council, headed by the Supreme Dalek. There have been various designs of both Emperor and Supreme Dalek over the years. But since the Daleks re-created themselves from a Progenitor Device, the ranks have been more easily discerned.

Supreme — the Supreme Dalek is predominantly white in colour.

Strategist – Dalek strategists are blue.

Eternal – the role of this Dalek is shrouded in mystery, but it is yellow.

Scientist – Dalek scientists are orange.

Drone – the rank and file 'soldier' Daleks are red.

Defeats of the Cyberman

The Doctor has encountered the Cybermen many times, and he has always defeated them. Here are some of the ways he's put a stop to their plans:

- When the Cybermen attacked a
  weather control station on the moon, the
  Doctor used the gravitron that controlled
  the weather to attack the Cybermen and
  shoot them off into space.

- The Doctor managed to seal the
  Cybermen back into their ice tombs on
  Telos and destroyed their Controller –
  with the help of a man who had been
  cybernetically enhanced.

- UNIT helped the Doctor defeat the
  Cybermen, who enlisted the help of
  Tobias Vaughn and his International
  Electromatics company to attack.
  The Doctor used a device called
  the Cerebraton Mentor, which used
  emotions as a weapon against the
  Cybermen.

- The Cybermen who attacked Voga,
  the planet of gold, were destroyed by
  a Skystriker missile.

- The Doctor used the sentient Nemesis
  statue as a weapon against the
  Cybermen who came to steal it. The
  Nemesis destroyed their hidden fleet.

- On a Parallel Earth, the Doctor
  deactivated the Cybermen's emotional
  inhibitors and they were unable to cope
  with the shock.

- The Cybermen who came through the
  Void, together with a group of Daleks
  and their Genesis Ark, were sent back
  into the Void by the Doctor.

- Some of these Cybermen escaped to
  London in the mid-nineteenth century,
  where the Doctor destroyed them
  together with their Dreadnought-class
  CyberKing warship.

Inhuman Nature

While some monsters are dangerous by design, others are merely acting on impulse and behaving according to their nature. The Stingray creatures that reduced the planet of San Helios to sand and dust were not deliberately out to destroy a great civilisation for some dastardly purpose. They were merely feeding, trying to survive. Here are some other creatures whose 'wickedness' is all down to their nature:

Isolus Child A stranded Isolus Child turned people into drawings. The Tenth Doctor and Rose managed to reunite the lonely Isolus Child with its 'family', once they had worked out it just wanted to play.

Krafayis The savage, invisible creature encountered by the Doctor, Amy and Van Gogh was acting out of instinct and pain when it attacked and killed. Whether – as in Gallifreyan legend – the Krafayis are blind and savage by nature, is not known for certain.

The Macra Once an intelligent race that enslaved others in order to get the gas they need to survive. By the time the Tenth Doctor encountered them on New Earth, they had been reduced to instinctive, unthinking animals.

Star Whale In pain and alone, the Star Whale that powered *Starship UK* was acting from instinct when it attacked.

Red-Eyed Ood The Ood are by nature passive and friendly. Those who suffer from Red-Eye are acting out of character – through illness, or because they were possessed by the terrifying Beast.

149

Defeats of the Weeping Angels

The Weeping Angels are renowned for being impossible to escape. But the Doctor and his friends have managed to defeat them several times. Here are a few hints and tips:

- Sally Sparrow managed to defeat the Weeping Angels by getting them to look at each other. Four Angels were trying to get into the TARDIS when she dematerialised – leaving them staring at each other, and therefore unable to move.

- When Amy was menaced by a looped recording of a Weeping Angel captured on a security camera, she managed to pause the recording at exactly the moment it looped back to the start – the only split-second when the Weeping Angel was not on the video.

- Infected by the Weeping Angel that had managed to get into her eye, Amy thought she was turning to stone and couldn't move. The Doctor persuaded her this was just an illusion by biting her arm!

- Although she had to keep her eyes shut, Amy managed to trick a group of Weeping Angels into thinking she could see and was watching them.

- The Doctor defeated the Weeping Angels on the wreck of the *Byzantium* by changing the gravity so they all fell and smashed in the caves hundreds of metres below

- Always remember: they're coming. The Angels are coming for you. But listen, your life could depend on this: don't blink. Don't even blink. Blink and you're dead. They are fast – faster than you could believe. Don't turn your back, don't look away, and don't blink. Good luck.

As well as being his time and space vehicle, the TARDIS is the Doctor's home. It should be impervious to attack, immune to danger, a safe haven. Very few of the Doctor's monstrous enemies have actually managed to get inside the TARDIS. Occasionally – as with Blon Fel Fotch Pasameer-Day Slitheen – the Doctor has invited them on board. But some have entered by force and with hostile intent...

Cybermen The Cybermen have got into the TARDIS on several occasions. Once, the Doctor destroyed a Cyberleader using the gold badge owned by his late companion, Adric. Another time, the Cybermen forced the Doctor and Peri to take them to their planet, Telos.

Daleks Although the Daleks pursued the TARDIS through time and space, and have tried to destroy it several times, we only know of one Dalek getting inside. That happened when the Ninth Doctor accidentally materialised the TARDIS around a Dalek on the Emperor's command saucer. The Dalek was quickly destroyed by Captain Jack.

Exxilon A savage native of the planet Exxilon attacked Sarah Jane Smith inside the TARDIS after it lost all power.

The Master The Doctor's old enemy, the Master, has gained access to the TARDIS – and even stolen it – several times. Another renegade Time Lord, the Rani, also got inside the TARDIS with her Tetrap minion, Urak.

Sontarans A group of Sontarans led by Commander Stor hunted the Doctor and his friends through the immobilised TARDIS when they invaded Gallifrey.

Sutekh Last of the powerful Osirans, Sutekh projected his mind into the TARDIS. He also took over the Doctor so that he could send the animated corpse of Marcus Scarman and a Servicer robot in the TARDIS to the Pyramid of Mars.

Bad Programming

In the same way that some creatures are unpleasant and dangerous by nature, so some robots have been programmed that way. Technically, a robot cannot be good or bad, it merely follows the instructions, the program, it's been given. Listed here are some robots that should be friendly and helpful, but were programmed to behave rather differently ■

The Heavenly Host Supposed to be helpful and informative to the passengers of the starship *Titanic*, the Heavenly Host robots were reprogrammed by Max Capricorn to kill any survivors of the meteoroid strike he engineered to cripple the ship.

Smilers The Smilers were information, assistance and teaching robots seated in booths on *Starship UK*. But they also kept the population from questioning the status quo, and could change from smiling, to frowning, in a moment.

Robot K-1 Built to replace humans in difficult and dangerous operations such as deep mining, or exploring alien planets, experimental robot K-1 was reprogrammed by its creator Professor Kettlewell to help the Scientific Reform Society in its attempt to take over control of Earth.

 Clockwork Robots The clockwork robots that tried to repair the *SS Madame de Pompadour* were not programmed to kill, but that was how they interpreted their orders – killing the crew to take part of their bodies to repair the components of the space ship.

Kraal Androids The Kraals planned to replace key figures in a Space Defence Station and the nearby village of Devesham with androids. They even built android copies of the Fourth Doctor and his friends Sarah Jane Smith and Harry Sullivan. The Doctor reprogrammed his own android to fight the Kraal leader, Styggron.

Sandminer Robots

The robots on Storm Mine 4 were reprogrammed by a scientist and roboticist called Taren Capel, to rebel against their human masters.

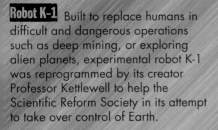

153

"The **Beast** and his armies shall rise from the Pit to make **war** against God."
Possessed Ood

"Location: Earth. Life forms detected. Exterminate. **Exterminate.** **Exterminate!** EXTERMINATE!"
Dalek Sec

Words of Warning

"We are Human Point Two. Every citizen will receive a free upgrade. You will become like us."
Cyberman

"We stare into the face of death!"
General Staal 'the undefeated' of the Tenth Sontaran Battle Fleet

"We would destroy the **Cybermen** with one **Dalek!**
You are superior in only one respect...
You are better at dying."

Dalek Sec

"Witness the crime.
Charge: physical assault.
Plea: guilty.
Sentence: execution...
Justice is swift."

Judoon Commander

"You are the **Doctor.**
You are an enemy of the **Daleks.**
You will be exterminated.
Exterminate!"

Dalek

"**The Angels are feasting...**
Soon we will have absorbed enough power
to consume this vessel, this world,
and all the stars and worlds beyond.
We will have dominion over all time and space."

Weeping Angel 'Bob'